Crocodile Snaps! — for Mark Gallant
Kangaroo Jumps! — for Jane Collier

Orchard Books, 95 Madison Avenue, New York, NY 10016

Printed and bound in Singapore

10 9 8 7 6 5 4 3 2 1

Library of Congress Cataloging-in-Publication Data

Lehan, Daniel.
Crocodile snaps!/Kangaroo jumps! / Daniel Lehan.   p.   cm.
Summary: In these two books in one (turn it over), a crocodile snaps and gets a meal,
and an unwilling kangaroo needs a birthday present before he'll jump.
ISBN 0-531-05484-5
1. Upside-down books–Specimens.   [1. Crocodiles—Fiction.   2. Kangaroos—Fiction.   3. Upside-down books.
4. Toy and movable books.]   I. Lehan, Daniel. Kangaroo jumps! 1993.   II. Title.
III. Title: Kangaroo jumps!   PZ7.L521553Cr   1993   [E]—dc20   92-50842

CROCODILE

SNAPS!

DANIEL LEHAN

Orchard Books
New York

CHASE

CHASE

SNAP!

SN

AP!

MUNCH

CRUNCH

YUM
YUM

KEVIN JUMPS FOR JOY!!

SURPRISE!

HAPPY

BIRTHDAY!

Boo!

Boo!

Boo!

Boo!

KEVIN
JUMP.

NOTHING CAN MAKE

SITS.

KANGAROO JUMPS!

DANIEL LEHAN

Orchard Books
New York